Because
everyone loves
a good story...

Alanna Max

To Jane, Milena, Amelia & Haris, who kindly feed our little cat
when we're away —A.McQ.

To Rosie, with love from Rosi — R.B.

Lulu does a great job of
finding out how to look after
her little cat.

If you would like to find out more about
cat care, go to CATS Protection's website:
www.cats.org.uk and click on Education
for information for teachers and kids.

First published in paperback in 2018 by
Alanna Max
28 Charteris Road,
London
N4 3AB

www.AlannaMax.com

PB 1
Printed in China

ISBN: 978-1-907825-170

Lulu Gets a Cat

Anna McQuinn
Illustrated by Rosalind Beardshaw

Alanna Max

Lulu loves cats.
She wants a real one.

Mummy says looking after a cat
is a lot of work.

Lulu decides to find out more.

She learns that cats are super
at smelling and hearing.

Lulu reads all about how to care for cats.
She pretends Dinah is a real cat
and practices looking after her.

Mon tues wed thurs fri sat sun

At last Mummy agrees. Lulu can get a cat!
Mummy and Lulu find out how to adopt one.

At the cat shelter, they meet Jeremy.
He shows them three perfect cats.

Before Lulu can decide, one little cat chooses her!

Jeremy says moving is scary for cats.
He gives Lulu a list of things that will help.

Lulu will be back as soon as
everything at home is ready.

All the next day, Lulu and Mummy shop.
What a lot of stuff for a little cat!

Lulu and Daddy make a special corner where her cat will settle in.

Finally Lulu is ready to bring her cat home.

But the little cat is afraid.
Her own blanket makes
her feel safe.

Lulu tells her not to worry.

At home, the little cat stays in the carry case. After a while, she comes out and sniffs around.

Lulu watches for now. She knows her cat isn't ready to play just yet.

Lulu decides to call her cat *Makeda*.
It is the name of an African Queen.

Lulu takes excellent care of Makeda.
She feeds her and gives her fresh water.

One day, Lulu's friend Tayo brings
a special present for Makeda.

Tayo and Lulu play with Makeda all afternoon.

At last Makeda feels right at home.
Her favourite thing is to snuggle Lulu!

Every evening Lulu reads to Makeda.
Tonight's story is about a famous cat.

Lulu loves her new little cat. And bed-time stories with Makeda are the best of all.

Praise for the Lulu & Zeki books

This belongs on the shelf with the holy books. Lulu is the cutest little girl in the whole world and this book celebrates the love of libraries and learning and books and stories. This book made me so happy I cried.

Anna McQuinn continues to capture the gentle, everyday moments of childhood.

An authentic, warm and positive reflection of toddler life. Let's find ways to get this book into every care setting, library and health visitor's clinic!

Hearson's cheery and warm illustrations are stunning.

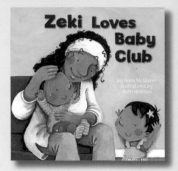

In the best picture book tradition, all Lulu's adventures are domestic ones, centred around family, home and the local community, because we all know how exciting these everyday experiences can be.

With gorgeous heartwarming artwork by Rosalind Beardshaw

Reflecting the everyday experiences of young children and highlighting things that really matter with little ones. If you live or work with kids under five, I think they should form an essential part of your library.

Anna McQuinn's stories of Lulu are authentic, and totally in tune with young children's lives – the interior as well as the external.

The roots of reading, along with matters of love and life, are happily married in this bright, uplifting, outstanding and important offering.

Perfect in every way. That's all you really need to know.

The lovely illustrations convey the tenderness and physicality of the parent-child bond.

The illustrations in this book are just PRECIOUS!

Alanna Books has a number of titles that are beautifully delivered, with a real understanding of children and parents.

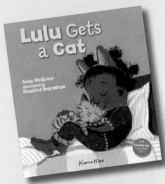

McQuinn has a real talent for creating stories that deal with childhood's important rights of passage and pitching them perfectly for the audience.

The Lulu books belong in every library, nursery and children's centre.

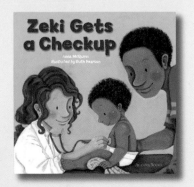

This book is everything good.

An instant hit with my little lady, sharing the book with her I could see how relatable young Zeki was to her. The sweet illustrations are so appealing and ooze cuteness. I think this book is brilliant.